KING ARTHUR

AND THE
KNIGHTS OF THE
ROUND TABLE

KING ARTHUR

AND THE
KNIGHTS OF THE
ROUND TABLE

Abridged from the original by

Benedict Flynn

Illustrations by

Young Ran Choi

CD narrated by
Sean Bean

SOURCEBOOKS
Jabberwocky
AN IMPRINT OF SOURCEBOOKS

If the CD included with this book is missing, broken, or defective, please email customer.service@sourcebooks.com for a replacement. Please include your name and address, and the ISBN number located on the back cover of this book.

Published by Sourcebooks Jabberwocky, an imprint of Sourcebooks, Inc.
P.O. Box 4410, Naperville, Illinois 60567-4410
(630) 961-3900
Fax: (630) 961-2168
www.sourcebooks.com

Library of Congress Cataloging-in-Publication Data

Flynn, Benedict.
   King Arthur and the knights of the Round Table / abridged from the original by Benedict Flynn ; illustrations by Young Ran Choi ; cd narrated by Sean Bean.
      p. cm.
   Summary: A retelling of the adventures and exploits of King Arthur and his knights at the court of Camelot and elsewhere in the land of the Britons.

   1. Arthurian romances--Adaptations. [1. Arthur, King--Legends. 2. Knights and knighthood--Folklore. 3. Folklore--England.] I. Choi, Young Ran, ill. II. Bean, Sean. III. Title.
   PZ8.1.F65Kin 2007
   [398.2]--dc22
                                    2007022804

                         Printed in China
                  RRD 10 9 8 7 6 5 4 3 2 1

Contents

Chapter 1

UTHER PENDRAGON'S SON IS HIDDEN

Uther Pendragon was dying. His only child with Queen Igraine died a baby. His knights already quarrelled over who should rule next. In the great fortress of Castle Camelot an old man slips unannounced into the king's bed-chamber. Beneath the furs that cover him Uther Pendragon is weakening fast. He has not moved or spoken for hours now.

"Pendragon," says the old man.

"Merlin! Is he safe? I must know. They must not discover him."

The old man nods. "Tell him, Merlin, when the time

comes, won't you? It was the only way."

Suddenly there is a noise, a rush of cold air. A woman enters. Her hair is wild and black and long.

"Too late, Morgana le Fay," says the old man. "Your magic has failed you this time. The Pendragon can tell you nothing now."

"My magic is not so dull, Merlin," she hisses at him. "I know about the child."

"But you shall not find him, Morgana. He will live to defeat you yet. Inform the queen, the king is dead."

Chapter 2

MERLIN RETURNS

Sir Ector's castle had deep dungeons and high towers, flying flapping flags, and a vast and very draughty hall for banquets. The fireplaces were large enough for Kay and Arthur to stand up in. But the lawless times since Uther Pendragon died made Castle Sauvage more than just a place where they could grow up and have fun. The Castle defended the villagers and the valley they lived in.

"No," said Sir Ector, stroking the white moustache on his big twinkling face. "We're not going."

"What?" said Arthur.

"But we've been summoned," Kay wailed. "A grand

tournament in London. At Christmas. We have to go."

"Great Council? Council of great thieves and great robber barons. We're not going."

"But every knight in the country will be there. And I'll be old enough to be a knight and joust by Christmas," moaned Kay.

"Exactly. Everyone will be there. It's most suspicious. All this about choosing a new king. We're not going and that's that."

He stormed off. Kay followed him.

"It's so unfair," Arthur thought. "I would be just as good a knight as Kay."

"I am sure you would, Arthur," someone said. Arthur turned around. He hadn't spoken out loud. And there had been no old man there a moment ago.

"Where did you come from?" he said.

"Oh, here and there," said the old man. He had a great mane of silver hair, and a very wrinkled face. Arthur stared at him.

"So what's unfair, Arthur?"

"Kay will be a knight by Christmas, but I will be just a squire. Sir Ector is my foster father. I have no noble blood. I practise just as much. And I'm better at most things. Now I'll spend all day polishing and rubbing."

The old man looked at him sharply. It sent shivers up and down Arthur's spine.

"How did he know my name?" Arthur wondered to himself. Arthur sat nervously while the old man took Sir Ector's seat.

"I knew you as a baby. It's fifteen years since Uther Pendragon died. So you must be fifteen."

Uther Pendragon, Arthur's father, took the name
"Pendragon" after seeing a dragon-shaped comet
overhead. It also meant "Chief Warrior".

"It's my birthday at Christmas, I'll be sixteen then,"
said Arthur. "But if you knew me as a baby, did you
know my parents?"

The stranger's furry white eyebrows lifted and fell.
"Indeed, I did."

But just then, Sir Ector flung open the door to the

Great Hall and marched in. Kay was still trailing behind him.

"Heavens," Sir Ector said, seeing Arthur and the old man by the fire. "Merlin!"

"The time is come," said Merlin, rising from his seat.

"Are you sure? So young?" said Sir Ector.

"Quite sure. I have studied the signs. Would you doubt Merlin?"

"No, no, it's just a little unexpected, that's all."

"Please," said Kay, impatient as usual. "What are you talking about?" Sir Ector sighed. "You'll find out soon

enough, Kay. In the mean-
time prepare my armour, and
your own. Arthur, take care
of the horses. We're going
to London after all."

Chapter 3

THE SWORD IN THE STONE

London was bursting with people. The summons to the grand tournament had gone to each knight in England. Each day the Great Council met to decide on a new king. But no one could agree as to who. Each day it grew more divided. Then, in a quiet churchyard not far from where the tournament was to be held, a huge block of stone appeared one morning. No one knew how it had got there. Set in the stone was a blacksmith's anvil, and thrust deep into the anvil, a great shining sword of steel. Running round the stone in letters of gold were the words: "Whoso pulleth out this sword from this stone and anvil, is rightwise born king of England."

The sword, anvil, and stone were rumoured to have appeared in a flash of blinding white light, seen only by one knight while deep in prayer in the nearby church.

Word spread quickly. Every knight had a try at pulling out the sword. Hundreds, because so many had come for the tournament. But everyone failed. The sword stayed firmly in its anvil. Finally the Great Council decided that since drawing the sword from the anvil was obviously impossible, it was a sign that they should not have a king at all. Eventually the day of the tournament dawned, crisp and frosty. Arthur spent the morning helping Kay and Sir Ector. Kay was so excited he could hardly ride. Arthur watched them join the crowd of knights heading for the tournament.

Later, Arthur rode slowly to the tournament ground himself. The streets were deserted now, all the shops shut up. Suddenly Kay appeared round the corner.

"Arthur! Where've you been? I've lost my sword. I can't fight without a sword. You'll have to go back to the inn and get another one."

But their inn was locked, shut. Now where would he find a sword? Kay has a better chance of borrowing one at the tournament ground. Arthur turned his horse again. But with the hurry to get back, and unfamiliar streets, he took a wrong turn, then another, and found

himself in a quiet square. And there, in a churchyard at one end, he caught sight of a shiny new sword.

"A sword!" said Arthur. "I'm sure nobody would mind if I borrowed that."

He grabbed the handle. The sword seemed stuck in an anvil. There was some writing on a block of stone beneath, but Arthur thought it better not to read it, just in case it said the taking of the sword was not allowed. He tugged at the blade. It gave a little, and then stuck.

"Oh come on," Arthur puffed, giving another heave. And then the sword came out as gently as from a scabbard. Kay had given up hope. Arthur threw him the sword. To his surprise

Sir Ector and Kay were standing together at the edge of the lists, where the knights jousted.

"What's wrong?" Arthur said.

"This is not Kay's sword."

"The inn was locked, Sir Ector," said Arthur. "It's the only one I could get. I'll take it back when you're finished."

"Arthur," Sir Ector said. "Tell me where you found this sword."

"It was stuck in an anvil in a churchyard. On top of a stone. I'm sure no one saw me take it. I promise I'll take it straight back."

"Merlin was right," Sir Ector said. "The time has come."

While they were speaking, a steady murmur was rippling through the crowd of knights milling around them. "The sword has been taken from the stone," they were muttering. Arthur began to wish he had never seen the sword. Had he done something really wrong?

"Could you find the place again?" Sir Ector asked him. Arthur nodded and the three of them pushed through the crowd. The churchyard was deathly quiet.

"This is the anvil," said Arthur.

"Put the sword back," commanded Sir Ector.

"I'm sorry, Sir Ector. I didn't realise . . ."

"Now pull it out."

The sword slipped easily from the anvil. Sir Ector knelt on one knee and pulled Kay down with him. "My lord," he said.

"My what?" said Arthur "Why are you kneeling, Sir Ector?"

"Arthur," said Sir Ector. "I am not your father."

"I know that, Sir Ector."

"You don't understand. Read the inscription, Kay."

So Kay traced the lettering with his finger and out loud read: "Whoso pulleth this sword from this stone and anvil is rightwise born king of England."

"Arthur," said Sir Ector, "that's you. Your father was Uther Pendragon. You are the new king."

Chapter 4

A WARNING FROM MERLIN

Not everybody was pleased that Arthur had managed to pull out the sword. At first the Great Council refused to accept it. "A beardless, low-born boy from nowhere? People will laugh at us!" they declared. "Let us wait until Easter. Some great knight may yet come and pull out the sword." But at Easter, the Council still refused to crown him.

"The Council has decided to postpone the coronation until Whitsun, to investigate the unusual character of the claim in more detail," the heralds declared.

But this time Arthur leapt on to the anvil.

"Enough!" he cried. "By this sword and my honour, I am Arthur, King of England. This is my pledge: to rid us of the Saxons, bring peace to my kingdom and uphold justice for all."

"King Arthur!" the people roared. "Arthur is our king. He has the sword. God has given him the right to rule us."

King Arthur may have been a real British king around the 6th century. There are references to "Arthur" in documents describing battles that occurred at that time and many archaeologists have looked for the legendary location of Camelot and Arthur's final resting place.

Their cheers carried to the ears of the jealous warlords of the Council. And when they heard it, they knew their rule was finished. Some decided to welcome him. Others fled far from Arthur deep into wild country, to gather a force to fight him.

Then Uther Pendragon's crown was laid on Arthur's head. He swore an oath to rule wisely and well, to right wrongs and give justice to everyone. One of the first things he did was to knight Kay. Sir Ector he made protector of his royal person.

The coronation feasts and festivals went on for days. When the celebrations were quite over, Arthur found himself alone in the throne room. He took off his crown.

"Heavy, isn't it?" He knew that voice.

"Merlin," said Arthur. "I was wondering if you might appear. But I don't understand. Why me?"

"It's quite simple," said Merlin. "You are the son of Uther Pendragon and Queen Igraine. When you were a baby I took you from your mother and father, and gave you to Sir Ector and his wife to be looked after. Everyone said you died of fever."

"Yes, but I still don't understand why."

"Your mother was married to someone before your father. You have three half-sisters, Arthur. All three are witches, but one is the most powerful sorceress I have ever known. She is your greatest enemy. Her name is Morgana le Fay. It was because of her I took you from your parents and hid you with Sir Ector. Had Morgana or her sisters reached you first, Arthur, things would be very different. Morgana's ambition is only matched by her wickedness. Your destiny is to struggle against her, Arthur. Now, Morgana's magic is rising; that is why your time has come. You will not be alone. I have powers of my own. But the heaviest burden is yours to carry. Against her, you are the people's strength and guide. You must not fail them."

Chapter 5

THE BATTLE AGAINST PELLINORE

So Arthur raised an army to reclaim his kingdom and bring peace to Britain. At first they were a rabble and the rebel lords of the Great Council were powerful. But the young king's courage, and each new victory, swelled their numbers. Knights and common people came flocking to his flag until they were tens of thousands strong. Arthur decided to make his capital at a place called Camelot. He built a hill-top castle to celebrate the beginning of a new era. Then word came of new enemies who refused to accept Arthur as rightful king. They had besieged an ally of Arthur's, King Leodegraunce, in his castle in Wales.

So Arthur's army in their thousands and their tens of thousands descended on Castle Cameliard to drive them out forever. Arthur himself led the charge, and, rebel knights and kings alike, they ran from him, scattering like sheep. All but one: King Pellinore stood his ground even when his allies deserted him. Pellinore was the most ferocious and feared of all the kings who defied Arthur. But Arthur had to defeat the rebel king to say his new reign had truly begun. The task was his alone to perform.

Pellinore's blade sang for Arthur's blood as he whipped it from the scabbard. Arthur matched him stroke for stroke. Hard steel clashed against hard steel. The sparks showered down. Suddenly Arthur felt the strength drain from him, and he fell to his knees. With one last despairing lunge he thrust at Pellinore. To his horror, the blade simply shattered.

Pellinore lifted his sword to finish him off. Arthur was sure he could hear the sound of wild cackling laughter nearby. But Pellinore's blade never fell. Instead the king toppled to the ground with a crash. The laughter became a shriek of fury. There was a sudden rush of wind and it ceased.

"Did I not say I would be there if you needed me?" said Merlin, emerging from the shadows. Arthur closed his eyes in relief.

"I felt so weak, and the laughter . . ."

"It was Morgana le Fay. Gone now, though she will be back, I'm sure."

In the many legends of King Arthur, Morgana le Fay is sometimes a misguided healer. Other times, she is a pagan goddess or a sorceress of great acclaim.

Merlin helped Arthur mount his horse. Then, together, they rode back to Camelot.

It was not long before Arthur was recovered from Pellinore's blows. And yet he was not happy.

"Merlin," he said, "the sword I pulled from the stone was shattered by Morgana le Fay. Will my kingdom shatter?"

"There was no magic in that sword, Arthur. It served its purpose. The time has come for you to wield another sword. Tomorrow we will seek it out."

But when Arthur woke the next morning, it was to the sound of a harp being played. Arthur saw the harpist through the open door of a nearby room, a girl so beautiful he felt his heart leap with the joy of simply looking at her. Honey-coloured hair fell across her face; long, pale fingers softly coaxed the music from the strings. She looked up and smiled when Arthur's shadow fell over her. He felt suddenly dizzy. There was a tug at his arm. It was Merlin.

"King Leodegraunce's daughter, Guinevere," he said.

"But how beautiful," Arthur murmured, as Merlin led him out of the castle into the morning. They set off down an ancient track.

"Now that the kingdom is at peace, Merlin," Arthur said after a while, "perhaps I ought to have a queen. I'd like to marry Guinevere."

Merlin stopped his horse and turned to Arthur.

"Guinevere? Oh, no."

"And why not? King Leodegraunce is an ally. And she is most beautiful."

"The future will depend on your choice, Arthur. I can only warn you. I must not reveal your destiny. But you

threaten Camelot,
your own life, with
Guinevere as queen."

"How could Guinevere
possibly be dangerous?"

But the wizard would say no more.
And Arthur knew he loved Guinevere
and no one else.

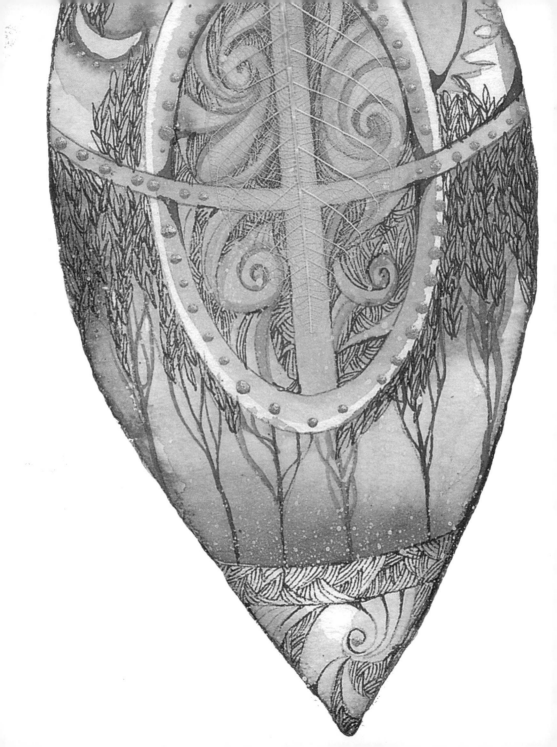

Chapter 6

THE LADY OF THE LAKE

Merlin led Arthur deeper and deeper into thick forest. Then plunging down into a hidden valley as the moon rose, they came upon a strange lake.

"Where are we?" said Arthur.

"A place of old magic, Arthur, the Lake of Avalon. We seek its guardian, Nimue, the Lady of the Lake, and the treasure she holds, the sword Excalibur. No one can resist its blow. It is yours, to serve your new kingdom."

Arthur stood on the shore.

"Tell her you have come," said Merlin.

"I am Arthur, King of England!" he shouted. "I seek the sword Excalibur."

The glassy surface of the lake rippled. Something rose from the water. The point of a blade broke the surface, then the blade glinted in the moonlight. Then, the hilt emerged grasped by a woman's hand. A woman dressed in flowing green appeared beside them. It was Nimue, the Lady of the Lake.

Ancient British and European folklore considered water to be the basis of all life, and water goddesses such as the Lady of the Lake were very popular.

"I have watched over Excalibur for a long time, Arthur," she said softly. "Now it awaits you. Use it wisely while you have it. Never be parted from it. Guard it as you would your own life. There are those who would use its power for evil."

She pointed to a barge which had appeared from

nowhere. "Enter in this boat. Take Excalibur, and be worthy."

Arthur stepped aboard and sat amongst the cushions scattered in it; the boat glided silently over the water. At the raised arm it paused, and Arthur reached for the blade.

Merlin stood alone on the shore. The Lady of the Lake had disappeared, but now the sorcerer held a scabbard in his hands. Arthur slid the sword into the scabbard and buckled a belt around his waist.

"So, now you have Excalibur, Arthur. Which do you prefer, the blade or the scabbard?" Merlin asked.

"The sword, of course," he said.

"Then you are wrong. The scabbard is worth ten times more. Whoever wears it can come to no harm. No wound can kill you, no potion poison you. However many you strike down with Excalibur, the scabbard will keep you safe. But look at the blade, read what is written there."

"Keep me!"

"Now turn it over," the sorcerer said.

"Throw me away! What does that mean?"

"Excalibur is not yours forever, Arthur, only for your lifetime. When death comes for you, you must make your way back here again and cast the sword into the water, back into the keeping of the Lady the Lake."

This time, they took a different route to Camelot. But Merlin seemed to know the way through. And then, as they came near to Camelot, Arthur found he was alone.

"What harm could I come to now? I have Excalibur and the scabbard," he said, and made camp. The crackle of the fire made Arthur drowsy. Soon, he would see Guinevere again. He could almost hear her harp strumming. She might have been there in front of him, the sound was so clear. And then suddenly, it seemed she was, as lovely as ever.

"Arthur," she said, kneeling on the ground beside him, "where have you been, my love?" She bent to kiss him. Beside them, the fire burned low, untended.

Arthur was falling asleep when his hand brushed the smooth hilt of Excalibur. And as clear as a hunting horn on a frosty day, its power sang out in his mind. The woman was not Guinevere. This was enchantment. Her hair was thick. Black, snaky strands tangling, binding him. Her kiss was sucking at his strength. Arthur struggled to escape; he dragged himself to his feet, swinging Excalibur around him. Too late: Morgana and her sisters were beyond its reach.

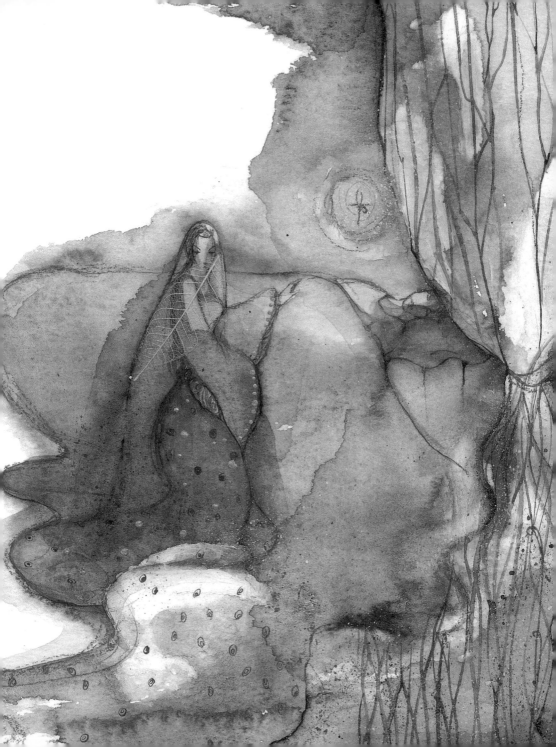

But out of the darkness came a sound terrible enough to freeze a man's blood. Once before he had heard it, but now it was three times as evil. Morgana le Fay, with her weird sisters, stepped out of the darkness. Morgana was clutching Excalibur's scabbard.

"Without this, Arthur," she cackled, "you will bleed as any mortal. I shall stand over you one day as you bleed your life-blood. Then your kingdom will be my kingdom." With that, the weird sisters disappeared. Then Arthur fell like a dead man to the ground.

Chapter 7

THE ROUND TABLE

Guinevere had not forgotten Arthur. And what joy when he discovered she too loved him. King Leodegraunce was more than pleased. "Of course," he said, when Arthur asked if he might marry his daughter. "If that's what she wants, too," knowing very well that it was. But Leodegraunce had a problem. What could he give Arthur as a wedding present?

"If he were anyone else, Guinevere," he said, "I could give him land, but he has more land than he knows what to do with. Of course, I shall send a hundred of my best knights to serve him, but—something different, something to mark the wedding properly."

When the wedding celebrations were over, Leodegraunce took Arthur into the great hall of the palace at Camelot. There, almost filling the entire room, was an enormous round table. Even Arthur, who could command the finest work in Britain, was impressed. Surrounding it were one hundred and fifty richly carved chairs.

"This table was your father's once, Arthur," said King Leodegraunce. "Merlin had it made for him, and when your father died, it came to me to look after. There is no other table like this in all England. Now it is my gift to you."

The modern English city of Winchester is home to a large round table thought by some to be the actual round table from King Arthur's day.

For a moment Arthur said nothing. He walked all the way round the table and back to where Leodegraunce stood.

"This table will be the foundation of my reign, Leodegraunce. Only the best knights will sit here. True knights worthy of helping me build a new kingdom, the kingdom of Logres. We must search them out and fill each seat. They shall be called the Knights of the Table Round. Every knight will swear an oath to protect the weak, show mercy to those who ask, and perform only deeds that do honour to the Table, the kingdom, and God. Your hundred knights, they shall be the first."

The doors of the great hall suddenly swung open. Merlin entered followed by a line of knights. They filed round the table and stopped, each one behind a seat. Arthur counted twenty-eight.

"I have searched, Arthur," said Merlin. "And these knights are worthy to fill the seats of the Round Table. Now, let us begin."

Leodegraunce called for his one hundred knights.
And the one hundred and twenty-eight knights swore
their oath, all burning to perform great deeds and prove
themselves worthy of Arthur's choice.

Arthur decided that at Pentecost each year the
knights would return to the Table, renew their oath and
tell what they had done to fulfil their vows. But for now
the first meeting of the Table was over. Merlin stood.

"Listen always to your King," he said. "There never was such a king as Arthur, nor will there be. Trust him, and Logres will be a place of light and happiness. Turn your face from him, and you will reap the whirlwind. Go," he proclaimed, "and bring all honour to the Table and to the kingdom of Logres."

Chapter 8

MERLIN DEPARTS

But just then a herald entered the hall and walked quickly over to Arthur and whispered in his ear.

"No, no," said Arthur. "Let them in."

An old man and his wife came into the hall. They were bent double by hard work and poverty, but behind them stood a young man with noble bearing, tall and strong.

"My name is Aries," said the old man. "I heard at this happy time King Arthur would grant a boon to anyone who asked him."

"This is true," said Arthur. "What do you ask?"

"That you make our son knight, my king," said his wife.

"I know the honour I ask, my lord," said the cowherd. "But I have thirteen sons. They harvest, herd and thatch for me, everything I ask, but this one, I cannot get a day's work from him. He only practises to be a knight."

Arthur looked at the young man. He stood upright and unafraid. "What is your name?" said Arthur.

"Tor, Sir."

"Well, Tor, I grant your boon, but it is a high ambition. In time, if you are worthy you may join us at the Round Table. Kneel now, and give me your sword."

Arthur touched him lightly on the shoulders with the blade.

"Arise now, Sir Tor."

Tor stood, and a gasp ran round the table. On the back of one of the empty chairs letters in gold had appeared spelling out his name. As they looked the names of other knights appeared, too. Arthur looked at Merlin.

"The truest knights the world will ever know will sit in these places," the sorcerer said. "Some are not yet born, some are already on their way here. But there is one whose name you will not know till he comes." He pointed to a seat. No name was written there, only the word: Perilous. "Only one knight may ever sit there. The best. He who dares and is unworthy shall be destroyed."

"Aries, you have lost a useless cow-hand, and I have found myself a fine knight," Arthur said.

Merlin did not stay for long after the first meeting of the Round Table.

"Arthur. This is our last meeting. I have come to bid you farewell, but I have one last word of warning for you."

"Leaving? Why? Where to?"

"A place as quiet as the grave to save the last of my strength for a struggle still to come. I will wake again, but far in the future. That time will be when Logres most needs me, in the mother of all battles. It is not enchantment that you must fear now, Arthur. It is those closest to you. Morgana le Fay will try to destroy you through them. And the greatest test will be on the field called Camlann."

Dawn was a long way off when the watchman on the main gate of Camelot saw Merlin leave. The darkness brought a visitor, too. In the morning, a serving girl discovered an abandoned baby boy, no more than a week or so old, but with dark hair already and startling blue eyes. Arthur and Guinevere decided to foster him themselves. They called him Mordred.

In the rustling gloom of the forests that closed round Camelot, Merlin was joined by Nimue, the Lady of the Lake. She led the way, until at last they came to a clearing, lit only by the white flowers of a hawthorn tree.

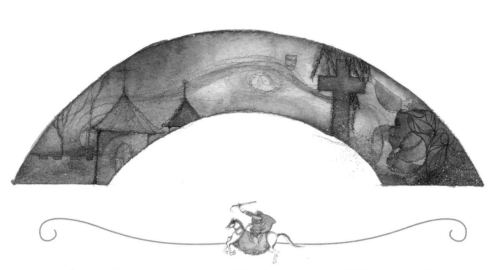

According to one story, Merlin once used his magical powers to transport several large stone slabs to England as a memorial for slain noblemen. Today that monument is called Stonehenge.

"So, this is the place," said Merlin. "But before I pass from the ways of men, Nimue, there is one last thing I must ask of you. Tomorrow, King Ban of Benwick will die in battle. Rescue his son and foster him until he is old enough to be a knight. His name is Lancelot. He and his son after him shall be the best of all the Knights of the Round Table. Do this for me, and Arthur."

As dawn woke the forest around them, Nimue made the ground open before her and guided Merlin down a narrow stairway, into a stone room. There, he laid himself on a great stone slab, like a table, and let out a sigh. His work was done.

"Rest now," said the Lady of the Lake. Then, with her magic, Nimue closed the passage and disappeared down the forest lanes.

Chapter 9

THE ARRIVAL OF SIR LANCELOT

One bright afternoon of spring, Camelot's drowsing was broken by a commotion in the castle court-yard. A knight, suffering from a terrible wound, had been carried in on a stretcher. Driven deep into his leg was the rusting, broken-off blade of a sword.

"My lord, help me," he said to Arthur. "I was told by a hermit that I would find a knight in Camelot who could draw out the blade from my leg. He would be the most noble and best of all the Knights of the Round Table."

Arthur had the knight carried into the castle. Then one by one, the Knights of the Round Table filed in to try and remove the blade. But each time, the broken blade refused to budge. "Your hermit must have been wrong," Arthur said to him.

Swords often had a mystical relationship with knights, as though each sword had only one true owner who could wield it. A knight who could remove a stuck sword was thought to have God's favour upon him and the sword was thought to be the knight's for life.

"No," said the knight. "He must be here."

"He is rambling, the poor man," Arthur was saying to Guinevere, when two horses came clattering through the gates. One of the riders was Nimue, the Lady of the Lake.

"Greetings Arthur," she said. "I bring you Lancelot, son of King Ban of Benwick. Merlin bid me foster him

since his father died in battle. I have prepared him to take his place at the Round Table. His time has come."

Suddenly, Arthur thought of the wounded knight. Perhaps he had come at just the right moment.

"Come with me," he said. "Your first test awaits you."

He led them upstairs. He made Lancelot kneel before him, then laid the flat of Excalibur first on one shoulder and then on the other. Lancelot promised him his loyalty. Then, he turned to the wounded knight. Arthur, Guinevere, and a little group of knights watched as he grasped the broken blade. It came smoothly from the wound.

"Look, the wound has closed," said Guinevere. "Lancelot has healed him."

Guinevere was entranced by the new knight. But the Lady of the Lake smiled sadly. The future had whispered her a warning, just as it had Merlin. This was the beginning of the end.

"Farewell, Sir Lancelot," she said. Then with a glance at Guinevere, she glided from the room. Arthur held up his hand for silence.

"So another seat is filled. Come, Sir Lancelot. Take your place at the Round Table. Fulfil your destiny."

But which seat? Would he be the one to take the seat marked Perilous? The other knights held their breath as he got closer and closer. He stopped. Not at Perilous. The gilded letters appeared with his name at a seat just one short.

At the next tournament Lancelot took on knight after knight. Each one yielded to him. Even Arthur found himself thrown to the ground at the joust. At the close of the tournament, Lancelot was presented with his prize, by Guinevere: a wreath of laurel leaves. Arthur was proud to have such a knight as Lancelot at the Table.

"To the victor the spoils," said Guinevere with a smile, placing the wreath on his bowed head. Lancelot looked up.

"And as a victor I claim my right," he said. "To be your champion, if you will have me. To fight for you and no other."

Guinevere slid a silk scarf from her neck. Her hands shook a little, as she tied it round his neck. Lancelot

bent his knee and kissed her hand. The crowd erupted in wave after wave of cheers.

"Champion, but of the loveliest of queens," he said so quietly that only Guinevere could hear.

Lancelot won the tournament year after year. No one could match him. But one day he suddenly announced he was going questing for noble adventure beyond Camelot. Arthur was sad to see him go, but Lancelot insisted. Guinevere watched from the castle walls until he disappeared into the distance, tears coursing down her face.

Chapter 10

LANCELOT AND THE GREAT WORM

From time to time, word would come of Lancelot's quests. But after a year or two, less and less news came to Camelot.

"Still no news of Lancelot," said Guinevere to Arthur. It was Pentecost, when knights from all over the country gathered at the Round Table.

"It's a year since we heard anything at all. I think we should send Percival and Gawain to look for him," said Arthur.

The two knights scoured the kingdom. But Lancelot seemed to have disappeared. Had they known where to look, the knights would have found him far from Camelot, in the Wastelands—rough country, where few people ever ventured. Two years and a day after he had left Arthur's court, Lancelot's questing brought him to a spring. He was drinking the water when a hermit appeared.

"Lancelot," said the hermit. "I have a quest for you." So Lancelot mounted his horse again and followed the old man, until they came to the Wastelands. The hermit turned to Lancelot. "See what the Great Worm has done."

Everywhere Lancelot looked it seemed a terrible forest fire had blown across the country. "Nothing can be grown," said the hermit. "The people are starving. They dare not leave their Castle. This is your quest, Lancelot, best of all knights. Kill the Great Worm. Only you g—"

A sudden roar drowned out his words. A huge ball of flame burst from the ground, followed by a vast worm, white and oozing. Tiny black eyes fixed on Lancelot. Another blast of flame exploded at him. Behind his shield and beneath his helmet, Lancelot could feel the heat shrivel his skin. He reached for his sword and stepped forward.

Lancelot woke with a sudden memory of the burning cloud that billowed from the monster's throat. He remembered hurling his sword like a spear at the monster. It must have killed the worm, or how else would he be in this room, with this girl looking down at him.

Lancelot smiled. "Is it dead, then?"

"Quite dead, thank you. You're in Castle Corbenic. I am Elaine, the Maid of Astolat," she said. "My father is King Pelles."

Every day, Elaine smoothed a salve onto his burns, until they began to heal.

"Much better," said Lancelot, one day when King Pelles asked him how he was. "I must leave you soon and carry on my questing."

Elaine felt her heart shrink inside her. She had fallen in love with Lancelot. How she pleaded with him not to leave. But Lancelot's heart was given to Guinevere. Finally, in desperation, she went to her father.

"Dry your tears, Elaine," said King Pelles. "He will indeed be your husband. The prophecy is written; so it will be fulfilled."

One morning, Brissen, Elaine's ancient nurse, brought a stranger to her bedchamber: a tall woman, with wild black hair and strange blue eyes.

"So," she said. Her voice brought a chill to the room. "You wish for the love of the noble Sir Lancelot. But you will never make him love you." She gave a little cackle. "Alone, that is. But perhaps with my help…"

Then Elaine stepped close. She and the strange woman talked in low voices so Brissen might not hear them. Elaine was clutching a tiny glass bottle tightly in her hand when the woman finally left.

Many legends feature potions that confuse, enchant, or hurt heroes. William Shakespeare included them in several of his plays and poems.

At supper that night, Lancelot spoke of his plans to leave Corbenic that very next day. King Pelles was sorry to hear it.

"The best wine then. A grand farewell for Lancelot!"

he shouted, and someone filled Lancelot's glass. The new wine tasted richer and spicier to Lancelot. When he drank it down it seemed to make him thirstier. He drained another, and another. It was close to midnight when he went to bed.

Lancelot opened the door to his chamber, feeling a little dizzy. But when he found Elaine already there, it did not seem at all strange to him. Nor that just then he realised that she was more beautiful than any woman he had ever seen before.

"More beautiful than Guinevere?" Elaine held her breath. Was the potion working?

"Guinevere?" said Lancelot. He could vaguely remember a woman who had that name. "Much more than Guinevere," he said. "Would you marry me, Elaine?"

Elaine smiled. "But of course, Sir Knight," she said.

Lancelot became a devoted husband. Time flew by without a thought for Arthur and Camelot. Yet when Lancelot rode out from the castle for any reason, Elaine would worry. How long would the potion work? Surely he loved her truly now. But she could not feel happy. Especially since she discovered she was going to have a baby.

Chapter 11

LANCELOT RETURNS TO CAMELOT

One day, returning to the castle after a long hunt, Lancelot heard a shout. And then another. Then the ringing clash of steel on steel. It stirred half-forgotten memories in Lancelot. He seemed to recognise a voice. The shouts were coming from just ahead, where two knights were fighting for their lives. They had been ambushed. Lancelot charged into the struggle. The robbers began to fall back, then suddenly they turned tail and galloped off.

"Our thanks," said one of the rescued knights to Lancelot. They took their helmets off.

"Sir Percival! Sir Gawain!"

"Sir Lancelot! But at last."

"Two years looking for me?" said Lancelot, as they walked the horses back to Castle Corbenic. "Is it really so long since I was at Camelot?" And like a thunderbolt the thought of Guinevere came crashing into his mind. All thought of Elaine vanished. Lancelot wheeled round his charger.

"To Camelot!" he shouted. And without a moment's delay, they set off at the canter.

At her spinning wheel in Corbenic, Elaine shivered. Something was wrong, she was sure. Lancelot had been away for hours. Then came the news Lancelot had been seen galloping furiously north in the company of two other knights.

"Knights of the Round Table, my lady," said the squire. The enchantment was broken. She had lost him.

The horses ate up the miles to Camelot. Lancelot could think of nothing but Guinevere as he galloped. They arrived at the gates of Camelot, exhausted, soaked, and splattered in mud. But in the great hall of Camelot, Arthur knew instantly who the third knight was, even beneath the grime.

"At last! They found you! Where have you been, all this time away? Tell us all your tales."

So after dinner, Lancelot told the Table the stories of the monsters and tyrants he had fought, and the magic

he had overcome; the rescues of women and children, villages and whole towns. But Elaine, and the time at Castle Corbenic? He barely mentioned them at all. For hanging on his every word, there in front of him, was Guinevere, more radiant than ever.

Guinevere is, of course, the legendary Queen of Camelot, the woman who loved two men: her husband, King Arthur, and his best knight, Lancelot. The way that she is described changes with almost every telling of the tale, which is fitting for a woman whose name means "The White Fairy."

In Castle Corbenic, Elaine became ill and thin. Brissen searched everywhere for the strange wild woman who had given her the potion, but the witch was nowhere to be found. Elaine grew weaker and weaker. The baby was born, a little boy. But the effort of taking care of him was too much. After he had been christened, he was looked after in a convent.

"When I am dead," she said to her father, "lay me in a boat and send it floating down the river to Camelot. Put this in my hand." And she handed King Pelles a note. Then she sighed and closed her eyes for the last time.

When Lancelot heard the news that a barge carrying a beautiful dead maiden had been seen drifting down the river that ran by Camelot, something told him who it would be. She lay on a bed of white flowers dressed in white, as if for a wedding. And in her hands was a letter. Arthur took it, broke the seal. He read:

"You left me without farewell, Lancelot du Lac, so I have come to make my last goodbye to you. I, Elaine, Maid of Astolat, who loved you, and who had no love in return. Pray for my soul, Lancelot."

Guinevere would not even look at Lancelot when she heard what the letter had said. After Elaine was buried she still refused to see him, even though he sent message after message.

At court, more angry looks were sent in Lancelot's direction. Was he worthy of the Round Table? He had deserted his wife, after all. Lancelot could only hold his head low as Arthur murmured his disappointment.

"There are those who say you should be stripped of your knighthood," he said. "There is no worse punishment."

Lancelot could say nothing in his defence. There seemed nothing he could do to win back favour with

Arthur or Guinevere. Just when Lancelot thought he could bear it no longer, an old woman came to court. It was Brissen, Elaine's nurse.

"My lord," she said, "news came to us at Castle Corbenic of Sir Lancelot. There's some as say he is accused of deserting his wife, but it's not true. Elaine loved Lancelot from the moment they met, but Lancelot's love was all enchantment. My lady said herself it would only ever be enchantment that would win his affection, he was that dedicated to his queen. I was there my lord, when the sorceress came with wild black hair and starey blue eyes. She gave the Maid of Astolat a love potion."

Arthur recognised Morgana le Fay immediately. "Will we never be rid of her?" he muttered.

So Arthur proclaimed Lancelot free of any taint of dishonour and Guinevere blushed with joy at the thought that Lancelot had been true to her after all.

"Forgive me," Guinevere said softly to Lancelot. "My cruelty was from the jealousy of love."

And yet
Morgana le Fay's
magic had worked
in unexpected ways.
Lancelot was forgiven by
Arthur, but Lancelot knew in his
heart he was unworthy of his
king. He was even more in love
with the queen now. And now she
loved him as much.

Chapter 12

THE ARRIVAL OF SIR GALAHAD

People wondered at Mordred, with his black hair and cruel pale blue eyes. Some noticed how he seemed to look like Arthur. Arthur had made him a knight while Lancelot was still lost in Castle Corbenic. But Mordred felt most at home in the hidden-away places deep in the forest.

It was just in one such place he came across a woman sitting by a pot bubbling over a fire. She had hair as black as Mordred's and long thin fingers ending in wicked nails.

"So Mordred," she said. "It is time we met. I have watched you from the day you arrived at Camelot. Before that even. I watched you being born." Mordred sat down. He suspected that he knew who this woman might be. "I knew your mother," she said. "More than that, Mordred. I know your father too."

And then, Morgana le Fay told him things he had wondered about almost every day of his life, the questions no one could answer before now— although perhaps, not as fully as she could have. She made no mention of enchantment, nor that she had planned Mordred's entire life.

"Arthur, my father? Are you sure?" said Mordred. His fists clenched. Morgana watched him intently. He would not fail her. The hate she planted all those years ago suddenly blossomed.

"So I am his heir," he said.

Morgana told him to keep silent. "The time will come," she said.

Mordred and Morgana le Fay often met in the forest after that. Together they began to plan.

That Pentecost a squire came panting into the great hall of Camelot during dinner, and said to Arthur, "Sir, the strangest thing has appeared—a great stone floating down the river, with a sword sticking into it."

So they left their dinner and rushed to the river. There, bobbing by the bank, was a boulder of red marble with a sword stuck in it. Engraved on the stone were some words.

"No man shall draw me but the purest knight of all."

"Lancelot," said Arthur, "that must mean you."

"No, no," he said, suddenly thinking of Guinevere and blushing deep red.

"Well who then?"

Back in the great hall they found a group of nuns led by an abbess. There was a tall young man with them. He carried himself proudly, like a true knight. It almost seemed he wore a suit of light, his armour was so polished and shining. But strangely, he carried no sword in his scabbard—only a shield, painted with scarlet.

"This boy was left to our care by his mother, who is dead," said the abbess. "He is of noble parentage and has been taught well in the use of arms. The time has come for him to take his place at the Round Table—to follow his destiny."

He stepped forward to stand in front of Arthur.

"He is Galahad, son of Lancelot du Lac and Elaine, Maid of Astolat."

The Round Table gasped and Lancelot stood up in astonishment.

"But the Round Table is full," said Arthur. "There is only the Perilous Seat. No knight has dared sit there."

But as he spoke, Galahad was walking round the Table. He stopped by the last empty seat. He lifted the silk covering of the seat. There, beneath, in gold letters, was his name.

"You cannot be a knight without a sword," said Arthur. "Come, I know the sword for you, and I will make you a knight with it."

So, for the second time, the court went down to the river where the boulder of red marble bobbed against the bank.

"There, Galahad," said Arthur, "take it from the stone." And without a second's thought Galahad leant from the bank and slipped the sword from its rocky bed. Arthur took the blade from him and knighted him at once.

Lancelot was overjoyed that his son had been chosen as the purest knight of all. But, he wondered, what would be asked of him? He did not have long to wait in finding out. Barely was Galahad's sword in his sheath, Camelot rocked with a sudden blast of wind. The candles blew out. Over the Round Table a light began to shine. It became a shape—a bowl or a dish covered by a silk cloth. It hovered there for a while, and then suddenly vanished.

"What was that?" asked Arthur.

"The Holy Grail," said Galahad. "The cup which Jesus drank from at the Last Supper before he was crucified. We are not fit to see it uncovered. The vision summons us on a quest. It is the greatest challenge: to seek out the Grail. If we are worthy, we may find it."

Galahad was to be the Grail Knight, the guardian of the sacred cup. Suddenly, Lancelot knew he too had to search for the Grail. Perhaps on the quest he might find forgiveness for his love of Guinevere.

No one knows where, if anywhere, the Holy Grail is today. However, several people in different countries around the world claim to have found it. Each "grail" has a different legend explaining its history from Jesus until it was found in modern times.

"My lord," said Lancelot, "I also wish to seek leave to quest for the Holy Grail."

"And I," said Gawain. Then, there was a chorus of voices around the Table. Nearly all rose and made the vow to seek the Grail, and bring it back to Camelot. Arthur was proud to see so many of his knights rise to the challenge. He looked at them round the Table.

"Tomorrow then," said Arthur. "You will begin, and may God be with you."

In the morning they all trooped out through the gates of Camelot. Then they split up in ones and twos, riding away from Camelot, some this way and some that, in their quest. Guinevere watched the knights disappear into the distance. She was weeping, but not for the Round Table. "But he will come back to me, I know he will. He must," she whispered in her heart.

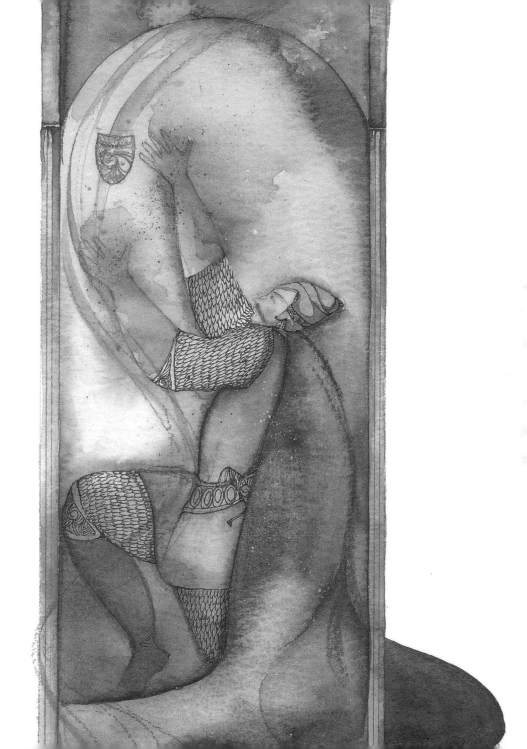

Chapter 13

THE QUEST FOR THE HOLY GRAIL

One by one the knights began to return home to Camelot. Some spoke of the death of knights they had travelled with. Some told of knights who strayed from the quest, tempted by earthly things. Some came back on foot with staring eyes, babbling of strange things and the prophecies of ancient hermits. All these things Arthur had written down in a great leather book.

Then there were only four still riding in search of the Grail: Sir Lancelot, Sir Bors, Sir Percival, and Sir

Galahad. After many months, their separate quests brought them by different ways deep into the heart of the Wastelands—to Castle Corbenic, and the end of the greatest and last quest of the Round Table.

"At last, some shelter," thought Sir Lancelot, as a little stone chapel emerged out of the blattering rain. "Any shelter is better than none at all."

But had he known where he was he would have moved on despite the storm. The door Lancelot hammered on was the door to the chapel of Castle Corbenic, but no one answered his hammering. So, wrapping his cloak around him he fell into an uneasy sleep in the shelter of the doorway. Just as Sir Lancelot's eyes closed, Sir Bors, Sir Percival, and Galahad opened theirs, to find themselves magically reunited in the Great Hall of Castle Corbenic.

King Pelles was happy to see the three knights, but the rest of his life was full of sadness. Elaine was dead. His castle had fallen into ruins. His land had become a windy desert. And most of all, he was in great pain from a terrible wound in his leg which would not heal.

When they had eaten, King Pelles bid them be silent. Outside the rain and wind had stopped. Quietly, the huge doors of the hall swung open.

"Now the end of the journey," breathed Sir Bors. In the archway was a maiden dressed in a white gown. She carried a silver candlestick with seven candles; behind her was another, carrying a silver spear which dripped blood from its point, ceaselessly, but the drips vanished before they hit the ground. A third carried a golden dish. Their hair flamed red, and their feet scarcely touched the ground as they walked.

"All this time," whispered Sir Percival to Sir Bors, "King Pelles has been the Guardian of the Grail."

Then a fourth maiden entered, so bright she seemed dressed in woven sunlight. She carried a small silver table, and on it something covered in white silk.

"The Grail Maiden," breathed Sir Bors.

"Our quest is nearly done," said Galahad. He joined the procession, it wound down the sweeping staircase of Castle Corbenic and led out silently to the chapel.

Something woke Lancelot, but he could not move; invisible hands held him back. He tried to speak; his throat seemed blocked. He could only watch as the Grail Procession marched slowly past him into the chapel. Then the doors to the chapel closed. Lancelot was left in the darkness outside.

Earlier Lancelot lived for some time at Castle Corbenic and never saw the Grail, because he was unworthy. Yet Sir Galahad, his son, would locate the Grail in that very same place. It is part of the Grail's power that only the most pure and holy of knights may even see it.

At the chapel altar, Galahad took the Bleeding Spear from the maiden who carried it.

"This is the spear of the Centurion who pierced Christ's side when he was on the cross. The blood that drips ceaselessly, and disappears, that is Christ's blood. Here," he said, letting a few drops fall into King Pelles's wound. Immediately, the gash closed, and the skin healed smoothly over, as if he had never received the blow.

"Ah, Sir Galahad! I have waited so long for this. Good Sir Galahad!" sighed King Pelles. And as the wound healed, the ruined towers of Castle Corbenic were magically rebuilt; leaves and flowers sprang to life on the trees round the chapel. The Wasteland became rich and fertile again.

Then, as the Grail Maiden took the covering of white silk off the Grail, Sir Galahad knelt.

"My quest is fulfilled, my life is complete. There is nothing more for me here," said Galahad, and put the Grail to his lips. A shaft of shimmering light, striking clean through the roof of the chapel struck him. As

Bors and Percival watched, Galahad seemed to disappear before their eyes. Outside, Lancelot saw the chapel brighten, and then plunge into darkness.

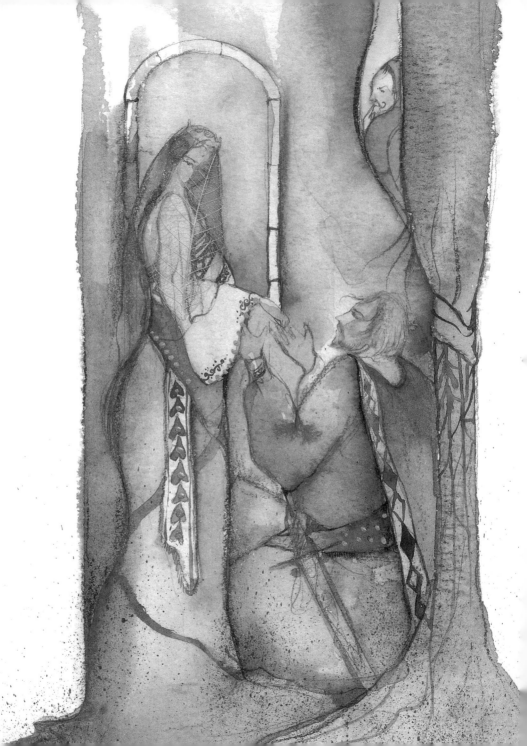

Chapter 14

MORDRED TRAPS LANCELOT AND GUINEVERE

At Camelot, Bors and Percival told the story of the Quest to Arthur and his queen, Guinevere, telling how Galahad had been taken to heaven.

"And Sir Lancelot," said Arthur, "you were there, weren't you?"

"I was too sinful to see," he said finally.

Arthur laughed. "Too sinful?"

Lancelot felt the weight of every stare boring into him. When he managed to drag his gaze from the table,

Mordred smiled, and he caught the look. He knew Sir Lancelot's sin.

Lancelot tried to stop loving Guinevere. And Guinevere tried to stop loving Lancelot. Meanwhile, Mordred had them watched at every moment. Then, one day, Lancelot and Guinevere went to take a walk with the knights and ladies of Arthur's court in the gardens of Camelot. Lancelot and Guinevere fell further and further behind.

"At last," said Mordred. "Quick now! Fetch Sir Agravain to me. Now we shall trap them."

But Lancelot and the queen had long gone when they arrived. And Mordred could only curse.

The next day, Lancelot and Guinevere went walking again with the ladies and knights of the court. This time they fell behind the company for a little longer. Mordred and Agravain only just missed them. The day after that, they were alone a little longer still. When they spent an afternoon alone together, Mordred knew

it was time to spring the trap. He paid Morgana le Fay a visit in the forest.

"Do you realise what you are saying, Agravain?" said Gawain, pushing his brother into a corner of the stable yard. "Telling the king would destroy Lancelot. The queen would have to be punished."

Agravain, meaning "arrogant," was one of Mordred's brothers. He was jealous and evil, willing to help Mordred expose Lancelot and Guinevere to make Arthur suffer.

"We have decided."

"Who is 'we'?"

"I, for one. The king will be told whether you like it or not."

"The king will be told what, Mordred?" It was Arthur.

"The queen and Sir Lancelot, my lord, are lovers."

"I don't believe you, Mordred. I trust my wife and Lancelot completely. Lies, more lies, Mordred."

Arthur wheeled his horse round and signalled for the hunt to begin. "What if I showed you proof, my lord?" Mordred shouted after him.

There seemed to be nothing to hunt that morning. Then Arthur heard the sound of laughter through the trees. It was faint, but there could be no doubt. It was Guinevere and Lancelot.

"After them!" shouted Arthur, clapping spurs to his horse. Mordred led the chase. But the laughter was like a will o' the wisp, always just ahead, leading them here and there. Only Mordred knew the laughter belonged to Morgana le Fay. Steadily he drew the hunt in a great circle back to Camelot.

"Look there," said Gawain. "Guinevere on the battlements." But as he spoke, he saw another figure join her.

"Yes," said Mordred, "Guinevere. And there is Lancelot. Proof, my lord, did I not tell you?"

Mordred galloped into the courtyard and scrambled up the tower to the battlements. But at the top, the tower door was locked.

"It is Mordred, Lancelot. We are betrayed!" said Guinevere in fright.

Lancelot was trapped. The door began to splinter from Mordred's battering. It crashed open. There were fourteen against Lancelot. But even together, they were no match for him. He used the doorway well, so that only two at a time could wield their swords effectively. Agravain died, and Gawain's younger brothers—ten knights altogether. Lancelot got clean away. But Guinevere was left behind. The punishment for adultery to the king was written—death, by burning.

"Proof, my lord if any more were needed," said Mordred to Arthur.

"Of what?" said Gawain. "This was your doing."

"Merlin tried to warn me, you know, Gawain," said Arthur, "the first time I ever saw her, but I wouldn't listen."

"Mark me well, my lord," said Mordred. "I shall kill Lancelot myself for this."

Chapter 15

THE SIEGE OF CASTLE JOYOUS

It was just after dawn, but Camelot's courtyard was crowded with people. Four of Mordred's men led Guinevere to a great bonfire of wood piled high round a stake.

"Poor thing, she looks so pale, so weak. And Sir Lancelot has abandoned her," murmured the crowd.

Mordred ignored them, and wound a chain round Guinevere and round the stake, tighter and tighter until she could not move. There was a final roll of drums. A firebrand was lit. But the tinder would not catch. The wood was damp with early morning dew. "Give me that!" said Mordred, snatching the brand. He thrust it deep into the pile. Only when white smoke puffed out did he stand back.

"Where is your champion, now?" he called to Guinevere. Suddenly, from nowhere, "Lancelot!" screamed Guinevere. "Help me!" And before anyone could move, Lancelot was on the burning pile beside her. His sword hacked through the stake, and the chains dropped away. And just as the flames were licking about their feet, he swept her into his saddle. And with a bound they were free.

Mordred and Gawain found Arthur in his chambers staring into the fire.

"My lord, the prisoner escaped," said Mordred. "The traitor Lancelot and a band of rebel knights took her."

Arthur did not look up, and Mordred could not see the tears of relief.

"I expect they have gone to Castle Joyous." He sounded pleased. Mordred was not.

"We will hunt them down," he said and went from the room.

"I do not want war," Gawain said. "Only I will revenge my brothers' death." The walls of Lancelot's castle towered above Arthur's army. The moat was as deep as the walls were high, and there was no way to cross it. No one could get in, but no one inside could get out either. Months of siege passed until one day Lancelot called to Gawain and Arthur from the great stone gate above the moat.

"No one has ever taken this castle, my lord. And nor will you. I have no quarrel with either of you. And I cannot kill my king and my friend."

"Then where is Guinevere?" cried Arthur. "Why is my kingdom at war with itself?"

But still Lancelot begged Arthur to make peace. "Never!" shouted Gawain and Mordred, and the cheers of Arthur's knights echoed off the castle walls. When Lancelot realised that nothing could prevent a battle, he blunted his lance and dulled the edge of his sword.

"Let no man lay a blade on the king or Gawain," he told his knights. And then they rode from the castle.

The sun was setting when Lancelot and Arthur came face to face. Arthur levelled his lance. His warhorse charged. When it seemed he must be run through, Lancelot lifted his shield. Arthur's lance was knocked away and suddenly he lay stunned on the ground. But instead of the killing blow, he felt a hand taking his, pulling him to his feet. Lancelot and Arthur looked at each other. Around them the battle roared on.

"Forgive me. Take back your queen, with honour. She loves you still."

Lancelot held out his hand. Arthur looked down at it for a moment. He thought of all the noble things Lancelot had done. The good things against the bad things. "I cannot draw Excalibur against you, Lancelot," he said finally, "in spite of everything. Take my hand."

"Prepare to die, Lancelot!" Gawain's hoarse shout came suddenly. But Lancelot's great clanging blow to his head dropped Gawain to the ground.

"Mordred. This business is over. Escort the queen to Camelot," said Arthur. "Go!"

Gawain brooded as he recovered his strength. Never once did he forget his oath to kill Lancelot.

Chapter 16

KING MORDRED

One bright morning, Lancelot looked from the parapets, and there was Gawain, in full armour.

"Defend yourself, Lancelot du Lac!" Gawain cried into the stiff breeze, "or die dishonoured!"

But when Lancelot wearily mounted his horse and rode out to meet him, Gawain was talking to someone else—a messenger from Camelot.

"My Lord," said Gawain to Arthur, "you must read this, Mordred's proclamation."

"Mordred?" Arthur unrolled the parchment.

"By the Grace of God, I, Mordred, natural son of Arthur, son of Uther Pendragon, heir to the kingdom of

Logres, hereby declare that King Arthur is dead. Long live the King!" It was signed Mordred, King of Logres, and all Arthur's other titles.

"The man had to sneak out of Camelot with this, my lord," said Gawain. "Mordred is raising an army."

But Arthur wasn't listening. Suddenly he was miles away, thinking of the first night he had Excalibur, and his dream of Guinevere. Mordred was his son by one of those witches! Of all Morgana le Fay's plans to take his kingdom, he never thought of this. How could he have been so blind to it? Would he never be rid of this troublesome witch?

Mordred and Morgana le Fay's plans are revealed, having set Arthur and Lancelot against each other with Sir Gawain caught in the middle, desperate to avenge the needless deaths of his family.

"Every knight and every soldier who can march, I want them on the road for Camelot at dawn tomorrow," Arthur roared.

Lancelot looked sadly at him. "I cannot fight with you, my lord. I have decided it is over for me. I will not wield my sword from this day on."

The following day, only Lancelot remained and, dressed now in the long brown robes of a monk, he watched the army march away.

Arthur rode again at the head of the great line of fighting men. This time, he had to rescue Guinevere.

Mordred smiled a crooked smile, "Everything is falling into place, Morgana. It will all be ours in a matter of days. With Merlin gone and Arthur out of the way, your enchantments will be supreme."

"Are you quite sure that no word of our plans has escaped Camelot?"

"The city is sealed tight as a drum, Morgana. Nothing comes in or out not checked by my men. The last of our allies have arrived. In the morning we march. Then we will destroy the Pendragon, once and for all. Surprise is on our side."

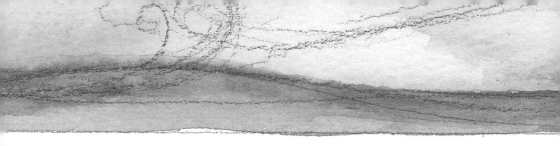

Morgana shifted in her chair. Her witch's thumbs prickled their warning.

"My lord, Sir Bedivere sends me."

Arthur nodded to the messenger. The army had travelled far and fast since leaving Castle Joyous.

"Mordred's army are not a morning's march from here—at a place called Camlann."

"Why does the name Camlann worry me so?" thought Arthur by the campfire that night. Was this the last great battle Merlin had spoken just before he disappeared? Would Merlin be there to help him? Then, as grey dawn touched the moor, he saw the dawn mist thicken into a shape. The Lady of the Lake!

"I come with a warning, Arthur," she said. "Fight Mordred tomorrow and any hope for the kingdom is lost. Knights will die in their thousands here. Promise Mordred what you like, make a truce, but do not meet him in battle. Save yourself and raise a great army to fight him another day."

Arthur tried to speak, but the mist gathered up the Lady of the Lake, and she disappeared.

When he woke, Arthur was not sure if the Lady of the Lake had really been there, or if he had dreamed what he remembered. But when Sir Bedivere showed him Mordred's camp, he knew she had been real.

"She spoke the truth," he murmured. Below in the valley of Camlann, Mordred's soldiers were camped far as the eye could see.

"We cannot fight them here. Both our armies would be destroyed," said Arthur. "If we fight, we die. Not just you and I, Bedivere, but thousands of knights. We must settle this revolt by talking. Go now, down to Mordred. Summon him to a parley."

It was not much later. Two great bristling lines drew up: Then, the banner for the parley was raised.

"Lift our own, Sir Bedivere, and we shall go and meet them at the ford," said Arthur. "Gawain, let no man take a step forward or throw a spear—unless you see a sword raised at the parley."

Gawain nodded grimly. Arthur spurred his horse into a canter.

Chapter 17

THE BATTLE AT CAMLANN

Well, my father, have you come to surrender?" said Mordred.

"I have come so that ten thousand knights will live tomorrow."

"Your knights, Arthur? I care nothing for them."

"As you wish, Mordred. But your knights will die too. I was willing to share my kingdom, but if I die today in battle, I promise you will be hunted down."

Arthur pulled the head of his horse round and set off to rejoin his knights. Mordred sat still in his saddle.

"No! Wait!" he shouted suddenly. The noise made his horse rear, and the crashing hooves disturbed a snake. Without a thought, Mordred's blade flickered

from its sheath. The snake lay in two. A sudden silence rolled down the valley. Arthur turned. He saw Mordred's naked sword. The ground began to tremble with the charge.

During a truce, every knight was required to keep his sword sheathed. When Mordred drew his sword, Arthur's army believed the truce was broken and charged.

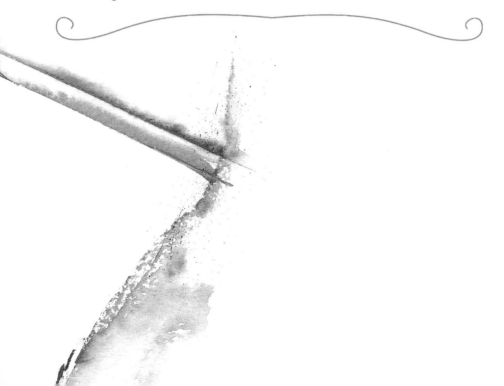

Arthur's kingdom died that day. The river Camlann ran red with the blood of his knights. As dusk fell, only a handful of knights remained on the field. Sir Bedivere was wounded but alive. And there was one other lumbering towards them.

"Mordred!" Arthur croaked. "Stand and fight!"

But Mordred did not want to fight now. Morgana le Fay had fled to some enchanted place. There was no one left to crown him, no knights to do him honour. Excalibur hummed angrily as Arthur swung it at Mordred's head. The weapons clashed. Then Excalibur's point seemed to catch in the ground. Arthur stumbled. Mordred saw his chance. He ran at Arthur. But Excalibur had been forged for this. The enchanted blade lifted free at the last moment, and buried itself in Mordred. Mordred met his doom, inches from Arthur's face. Sir Bedivere found his king crushed beneath Mordred.

"Bedivere, I am dying. Carry me to those woods. There is something I must do before I die."

Bedivere stumbled from the field to the edge of the wood, and placed Arthur carefully against a tree.

"I cannot carry you any further. I am too weak."

"You must go in my place then," said Arthur. "Here, take Excalibur. Go to the lake and throw it in."

"Where is the lake?"

"Beyond those trees."

Bedivere struggled to his feet and limped away. There was no lake near here. Throw away Excalibur? Arthur's mind must be wandering.

Then through the leaves he caught a glimpse of moonlight shining on water. How had Arthur known? Bedivere grasped Excalibur by the point to sling the sword from the shore. What if Arthur recovered? What if he needed it again? So Bedivere hid the sword, and went back to Arthur.

"Did you throw it?" Arthur's voice was fading now.

"It's gone," said Bedivere.

"What did you see?"

"It fell with a splash, and the lake swallowed it."

"Then you do not speak the truth, Bedivere. Go back and throw Excalibur into the lake."

So Bedivere returned to where he had hidden the sword. Such a noble sword. If Arthur died, Excalibur would be all that remained of his reign. He shoved it back.

"What did you see, Bedivere?"

"The ducks scattered, and the water rippled across the lake."

"Liar! Bedivere, must I do it myself?"

"No, no, no, my lord," said Bedivere. He turned, and went back to the lake. This time, he threw Excalibur as far as he could over the water. As the blade flashed in the moonlight over the lake, a woman's hand broke the surface. It caught the hilt of Excalibur and drew it down. Bedivere watched, amazed.

"Well?" said Arthur.

"A hand, my lord, reached out and caught Excalibur," said Bedivere.

"Well done, Bedivere," said Arthur, and let out a great sigh.

The trees parted, and Bedivere saw three ladies gliding towards him, veiled in black. They picked up Arthur as if he were no more than a child, and carried him to the barge they had arrived in.

"Where are you taking him?" asked Bedivere.

"To the Isle of Avalon," they answered. "His wound will be healed there, and then he will sleep until he is needed again."

Then the barge floated away into the darkness and the mist. But King Arthur was never forgotten, and he lies somewhere to this day, sleeping, but ready with Merlin for the call to save his land in its hour of greatest need. Just for now then, the tale ends of Arthur, Once and Future King.

ABOUT THE STORY AND AUTHOR

The story of *King Arthur and the Knights of the Round Table* has been told many times, by many different authors. First there were legends, passed from knight to knight in tales around the campfire or dinner table. Sir Thomas Mallory was one of the first to collect all these stories into one book. His *Le Morte d'Arthur* (French for "The Death of Arthur") was published in 1485. Many other versions followed, including *The Once and Future King* by T. H. White in 1958, and a series of books by Marion Zimmer Bradley, starting with *The Mists of Avalon* in 1979.

The Sourcebooks Jabberwocky edition of *King Arthur and the Knights of the Round Table* was written by Benedict Flynn, who has also written *Robin Hood*, *The Tale of Troy*, and *The Tale of Odysseus*.

THE SECRET GARDEN

Frances Hodgson Burnett

Told by Jenny Agutter

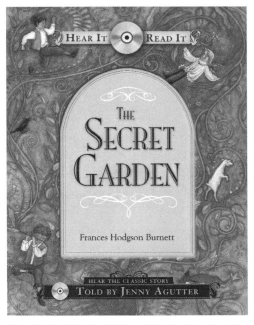

Mary Lennox doesn't want to move to England to live with her uncle, but she has no choice. At first she hates her uncle's cold house, the gardens and moors that surround it, and the servants with their funny way of talking. And at night, she hears a child crying, but the servants insist it's only the wind. Curious in spite of herself, Mary wanders the house and gardens and discovers that both are full of secrets.

$9.95 U.S/$11.95 CAN/£6.99 UK

ISBN-13: 978-1-4022-1244-4
ISBN-10: 1-4022-1244-5